BOOK 1

NANCY CLANCY
Super Sleuth

BOOK 1

NANCY CLANCY

Super Sleuth

WRITTEN BY
Jane O'Connor

ILLUSTRATIONS BY
Robin Preiss Glasser

HARPER

An Imprint of HarperCollinsPublishers

For my superb mother-in-law, Marge O'Connor
—J.O'C.

For Aaron: alias, Mr. Dude
—R.P.G.: alias, A.O.

Library of Congress Cataloging-in-Publication Data
O'Connor, Jane.
  Nancy Clancy, super sleuth / by Jane O'Connor ; illustrations by Robin
Preiss Glasser. — 1st ed.
    p.   cm. — (Fancy Nancy)
  Summary: In her chapter book debut, Nancy Clancy must find the culprit
when a prized possession goes missing at school.
  ISBN 978-0-06-240364-3
  [1. Mystery and detective stories.   2. Lost and found possessions—Fiction.
3. Schools—Fiction.   4. Vocabulary—Fiction.]   I. Preiss Glasser, Robin, ill.
II. Title.
PZ7.O222Nan 2012   2011044625
[Fic]—dc23   CIP
                                                                             AC
Typography by Jeanne L. Hogle
16 17 18 19   CG/RRDH   10 9 8 7 6 5 4 3 2
❖
Bind-up edition, 2015

CONTENTS

CHAPTER 1

HARDLY A MYSTERY

Nancy Clancy was all set to solve a mystery. She had a fancy magnifying glass complete with rhinestones. She had a spiral notepad and a flashlight. She had sunglasses, a hat with a floppy brim, and a pink trench coat. (A trench coat was the kind of raincoat that detectives wore.) She had superb detective skills. She was naturally nosy. So she was good at snooping. (Investigating was the professional word for snooping.)

Really the only thing Nancy was missing was a mystery.

"If only more criminals lived around here," she said to her father. He was at the kitchen table reading the Sunday sports pages.

"What?" he said without looking up.

"Nobody ever gets kidnapped. I bet there's never been a jewel heist." Then, in case her dad didn't know, Nancy added, "That means a jewel robbery."

Nancy sighed. "I wish we lived someplace like River Heights." That was where Nancy Drew lived. Nancy loved the Nancy

Drew books. She had read five so far. "In River Heights, criminals are lurking around every corner."

"Mmmmm. Sounds fun," her dad murmured.

Nancy's mother came into the kitchen. Nancy's little sister trailed behind her. She had on blue flippers that made a slapping sound as she walked.

"Have either of you seen JoJo's snorkel mask?" Nancy's mom asked.

Nancy's little sister hardly ever took off her snorkel mask or flippers. JoJo and her friend Freddy liked to pretend they were deep-sea divers searching for buried treasure.

Nancy's mom poured herself coffee. "We've looked everywhere. It's a mystery where it went."

Mystery! Nancy just heard the magic word. Okay, so it wasn't a big-deal mystery. But all great detectives had to start somewhere. She spread her arms. "Ta-da! Nancy Clancy, Super Sleuth, at your service."

"Aw, honey." Her mom smiled. "You'll look for it?"

"Sure. My rates are very reasonable." Nancy paused. "Only kidding. You're family. So my services are free."

Nancy went and slipped on her pink trench coat. It was important to dress like a professional. "JoJo, I just need to ask you a few questions," she said, pulling the

4

notepad from her pocket. "Trust me. We'll get to the bottom of this."

At that moment, Bree appeared at the back door. She was wearing a trench coat too. (Hers was purple.)

"JoJo left this at our house." Bree was holding a snorkel mask.

"Thanks!" Nancy's mom said. Then she turned to Nancy. "Sorry, sweetie."

Nancy scowled. Her first case was closed before it even got opened.

"I have to pick up a book for my mother. It's at the twins' house," Bree told Nancy. "Come with me."

CHAPTER 2

SNOOPING

The book for Bree's mom was in the Polskys' mailbox. Nancy and Bree were about to walk back home when Bree held a finger to her lips. "Shh. Listen."

Nancy could hear the Polsky twins arguing in their backyard.

"No fair!" Wanda shouted. "I get to pitch now."

7

"No! It's still my turn!" Rhonda said.

"Is not!"

Rhonda and Wanda were a year younger than Nancy and Bree. They were both superb at sports and very nice—except to each other. They got into lots of fights. Not just yelling fights, but hitting fights.

"Let's investigate!" Nancy said. She looked around. "The coast is clear!"

The girls dropped to their knees and crawled to the side of the twins' house. They tiptoed along the wall, their backs pressed flat against it. Silent as cats, they stopped at the back porch and hid behind an outdoor grill. Neither twin had spotted them. It was like Nancy and Bree were invisible. They smiled and high-fived each other.

"Here comes my fastball." Rhonda

started spinning her arm around like a pinwheel.

"I quit." Wanda threw down her mitt. "I'm not playing anymore." She started to stomp off.

Rhonda spun her arm around once more and let go of the ball.

Just in time, Wanda saw the ball whizzing right at her. She sprang forward to catch it.

Oops! She missed.

Double oops! She stumbled and landed facedown on the ground.

Ooh! That had to hurt! Nancy peeked over the top of the grill. "Wanda's bleeding!

She split her lip."

"I can't look." Bree stayed hunched down. She hated the sight of blood.

Nancy watched Wanda pull herself up. She was crying. Blood was all over her mouth and chin. Her hands, too. Wanda looked like something out of a horror movie!

"You did that on purpose!" Wanda yelled at Rhonda. "I'm gonna get you back. I'm—I'm gonna tell Nancy what you did the other day!"

Rhonda froze for a second.

Nancy did too.

"You swore you wouldn't tell!" Rhonda shouted.

"Tough. I'm telling Nancy."

Nancy wanted to pop up from behind the grill and shout, "Tell me what?" But Bree grabbed her by the arm and yanked her down.

"We're snooping, remember?" Bree hissed.

A moment later, the twins' dad appeared on the back porch. He looked mad. "Are you two fighting again?" he said. Then he took each of them by the arm and marched them inside the house.

CHAPTER 3

THE PLOT THICKENS

"So? What is Rhonda scared I'll find out? What secret has Wanda been keeping?" Nancy made her voice go soft and spooky. "It's the secret of the twins." She giggled. "Doesn't it sound like a Nancy Drew mystery?"

The girls were in Nancy's backyard at

Sleuth Headquarters. When they grew up, they planned to open a detective agency together. It would be called Partners in Crime Fighting. They had made superb business cards already.

"Maybe Rhonda spread a mean rumor about you," Bree said. "Like you smell or have cooties."

"Rhonda's my friend. What motive would she have?" Ooh la la! Nancy felt all tingly just saying the word "motive." It meant the reason for doing something bad.

"W-e-l-l." Bree drew the word out, like she was thinking really hard. "Maybe you did something mean to Rhonda and she's paying you back."

Nancy shook her head. "I didn't do anything."

"Maybe it's something you don't even realize you did. But it got Rhonda mad. Really mad."

"And so now Rhonda is seeking revenge?" Nancy added.

Bree nodded.

Double ooh la la! Nancy's eyes lit up. There was something thrilling about this idea. "Maybe she's set up a booby trap to get me!" Nancy pictured Rhonda digging a deep hole in her yard and covering it with grass and branches. As soon as Nancy walked over it, she'd plunge into darkness. No one would hear her cries for help.

Suddenly Nancy heard her mother calling her.

"Nancy, are you in the clubhouse?"

Nancy stuck her head out. "Mom, I told you before. It's not our clubhouse anymore. It's Sleuth Headquarters."

"Sorry. I forgot. Have you finished your paragraph for tomorrow?"

"Um, not exactly," Nancy answered.

"Have you started it?"

"Um, not exactly."

"Bree, I'm afraid you'll have to go home, and Nancy"—Nancy's mother pointed to the house—"get cracking!"

Nancy headed to her room. Nancy Drew

was so lucky. She never had to drop a case because of homework.

Tomorrow Nancy and all the other kids in her class had to bring in something special. "A memento" was what her teacher, Mr. Dudeny, had called it. The memento couldn't be a video game or a new pair of sneakers. A memento needed to be something personal, like a photo of a dead person in your family from long ago.

"Write a paragraph about what the memento means to you. But don't sign your name," Mr. Dudeny said. "Keep it a secret. We'll have fun guessing who each memento belongs to."

"Oh! So they'll be mystery mementos," Nancy said.

"Exactly," Mr. Dude told her. "I'm

bringing something too. Then on Tuesday all the mystery mementos will be on display for Family Day."

Nancy planned to bring *The Witch Tree Symbol,* which was a Nancy Drew book. It was special because long ago it had belonged to Nancy's neighbor, Mrs. DeVine. On the cover Nancy Drew looked different. Her clothes and hairdo were old-fashioned.

The only problem was that Nancy wanted her memento to be unique—something nobody else had. What if Bree's mystery memento was the Nancy Drew book that Mrs. DeVine had given *her?* Bree had already written her paragraph days ago. She never left homework for the last minute.

So Nancy sent a message to Bree in their Top-Secret Special Delivery mailbox. It was a basket on a rope strung between Nancy's bedroom window and Bree's.

What is your memento? She wrote the message in secret code. Only the two of them knew it. They needed a secret code if one of them was ever in danger and had to send for help. Nancy rang a bell to let Bree know mail was coming. Then she

Uqtta. Ot. F
vqnf wu pqv
vq vgnn.
                —Bree

pulled the rope until the basket reached Bree's window.

A few minutes later, a message came back. Bree's was in secret code too. It took Nancy a while to understand it. (In secret-code talk that was called deciphering a message.)

Bree had written: *Sorry. Mr. D told us not to tell.*

THE SECRET CODE EXPOSED! (Shhhhhhh!!!)

A = C	E = G	I = K	M = O	Q = S	U = W	Y = A
B = D	F = H	J = L	N = P	R = T	V = X	Z = B
C = E	G = I	K = M	O = Q	S = U	W = Y	
D = F	H = J	L = N	P = R	T = V	X = Z	

20

Ooh, Bree could be exasperating some-times!

Nancy thought about writing another message. But writing in code took so long. Of course, she could just pick up the phone or open the window and shout. Nancy would say, "Can you just tell me if you're bringing a Nancy Drew book? I am only asking because I don't want to bring in the same thing!"

But it wouldn't do any good. Bree was obstinate—that meant stubborn. In the end, Nancy decided to bring in a sparkling chunk of rock that looked like gold. She wanted kids to have a hard time figur-ing out who it belonged to. So when she wrote her paragraph, Nancy disguised her handwriting.

This glittering rock is called pyrite. Another name for it is fool's gold. That's because it looks like genuine gold. Long ago in days of yore, miners would find a chunk and think they had struck it rich. The joke was on them. Pyrite is not worth a lot of money. But it is still magnificent. I chose this memento because it was a present from my best friend, Bree. She bought it in a gift shop at a famous science museum in New York City.

It was quite a superb paragraph, if Nancy did say so herself. She had used vivid, interesting words. Mr. Dudeny would like that. Then something caught Nancy's eye. In one sen-tence there was a dead giveaway. Everyone would know Nancy had written it. Quickly she erased the words "my best friend, Bree." Instead she wrote "an acquaintance of mine."

Nancy put the rock and her paragraph in her backpack.

Not even five minutes later, the mail bell rang again.

Bree's message said, *I just saw the twins drive off with their parents. We can go back and snoop in their yard. Maybe we'll find the booby trap!*

Nancy grabbed her trench coat. Bree was already waiting for her on the sidewalk.

Bree whistled on the way over to the twins' house. Whistling was a superb detective skill. It made it seem like they were just out for some fresh air. No one would ever suspect they were snooping.

At first glance, the twins' yard looked the same as it had this morning—grass, trees, a swing set in back, lots of sports stuff everywhere. Nancy, however, was very observant. That meant she noticed stuff that other people didn't. Noticing stuff was also a superb detective skill. It kind of made up for not being able to whistle.

What Nancy noticed now was a pile of

branches near the swing set.

"Bree, look, a clue! I bet those branches are left over from when Rhonda made the booby trap!"

Bree clutched Nancy's arm. "Oh! I'm getting chills!"

A couple of large leaf rakes were on the porch. "I have an idea," Nancy said.

By pushing the rakes in front of them up and down the yard, the girls would spot the hidden trap before either of them fell into it. Unfortunately, the yard was pretty big. They hadn't covered much ground when they heard a car. It was pulling into the twins' driveway!

Bree and Nancy dropped the rakes and scrammed. They ran through the lilac bushes in between the twins' house and

Mrs. DeVine's. They dashed across Mrs. DeVine's yard, wiggled through the hedge that separated her yard from Nancy's, and hid inside Headquarters.

Whew! That was a close call. But they were safe! They collapsed into the bean-bag chairs.

"You really think there's a booby trap?" Bree asked. She sounded doubtful now.

"More and more, I'm sure of it. We need to search that whole yard. But let's sneak back under cover of darkness." That meant at night but sounded way more

dangerous. They'd have to use flash-
lights. There'd be spooky night noises.
Nancy could picture it all!

"We're not allowed out after dark," Bree
pointed out.

Nancy knew that. She just didn't want
to be reminded of it. Not right now. It was
more fun picturing the two of them sneaking around in the dark.

Nancy sighed. It was awfully difficult to
be a glamorous detective when your bedtime was eight thirty.

CHAPTER 4

MYSTERY MEMENTOS

*T*he cowboy hat is Robert's memento, Nancy wrote. She was filling in the blanks on her Mystery Memento sheet. Mr. Dudeny had handed a sheet to each kid. Then he said, "Go to it, Dudes."

All the mystery mementos were on a table by the windows.

The cowboy hat was easy. Robert used to live in Texas.

The glass mouse is Bree's memento, Nancy wrote.

Bree owned lots of tiny glass animals. She kept them on a special shelf in her room. *See? I knew right away. You could have told me.* Nancy didn't say those words out loud. She just thought them. Nancy figured that sometimes she and Bree could read each other's minds.

Two kids had brought in shells. One was white with brown specks. The other was white and purple. *The white-and-brown shell is Clara's memento,* Nancy wrote. Clara had not disguised her handwriting.

The paragraph for the other shell was typed. It said, *I found this shell on a beach in Florida. We stayed at a hotel with three pools. My family had a suite. Suites are bigger and cost more than regular hotel rooms. I had the best time ever in Florida.*

The white-and-purple shell had to belong to Grace. Grace bragged all the time about her trip to Florida.

"Hey! No fair, you're peeking!" Nancy said. Grace was sneaking a look at her sheet.

"I'm not! I guessed yours already," Grace said. "It's the bead bracelet."

"Maybe yes, maybe no." Nancy smiled. *Ha-ha! You are sadly mistaken. That's fancy for wrong, wrong, wrong!* Nancy didn't say this out loud either. She was not friends with Grace. Grace would never be able to read her mind.

Nancy went around the table. Hmmm. Who did the snow globe with the Statue of Liberty belong to? And what about the shark teeth? Or the swim trophy from Sighing Pines Day Camp? Nancy was stumped. She stopped at a big deep-blue marble. Bree was looking at it too. Inside it was a white swirl. The marble was taped to the table so it wouldn't fall off.

"Whose is it, you think?" Nancy said

to Bree and Clara.

"It's gorgeous," Clara said. "That's my favorite color blue."

"I bet I know who it belongs to," Grace said. "But I'm not telling."

Nancy ignored her. "It looks like a precious jewel." Nancy held up her hand and imagined the marble was a fancy ring on her finger. Then she read the paragraph.

My grandfather gave me this. He taught me how to play a game with marbles. It's a lot of fun, and I got pretty good at it. When he was a boy, all his friends played the game together. But most kids today don't know how. I can teach everybody the rules.

The paragraph talked about teaching. Was that a clue? Hmmm. Nancy tapped her pencil eraser against her lip. Maybe the marble belonged to Mr. Dudeny.

At the end of the day, the kids revealed which mementos were theirs.

"Mine is the potato that looks like a witch's head," Lionel said.

"I knew it!" lots of kids said at once. Nancy had guessed right too. Lionel was such a goofball.

Besides Bree, only Robert and Tamar figured out Nancy's memento. The other kids probably figured she'd bring in something fancier.

Mr. Dudeny went last. "I brought in the marble."

"Superb!" Nancy punched her fist in the air. "I guessed it was yours, Mr. D."

Grace said, "I got thirteen right. That's really good, isn't it, Mr. Dude?"

"This isn't a test," Mr. Dudeny said. "Guessing was just for fun. Your paragraphs are enthralling. That means I found them very, very interesting. So, Dudes? Want to learn how to play marbles?"

Everybody crowded around Mr. Dudeny while he drew a chalk circle on the floor.

In the middle he made a plus sign with thirteen smaller marbles.

He held up the big blue marble. "This is the shooter. It shoots the little marbles."

"Hey, I'm a marble. Ooh! Ooh! I got shot!" Lionel clutched his chest and staggered around.

"If you shoot a marble outside the circle, you get a point," Mr. D explained. "The player with the most points wins.

I used to be pretty good."

He bent down on one knee. He put his blue shooter outside the circle. A flick of his thumb sent it whizzing toward the little marbles. Three got hit. When they stopped rolling, two were outside the circle.

"Ooh. Can we try?" Robert asked.

Mr. Dudeny said, "It just so happens I brought a bunch of shooters." He started handing them out. Robert got one with orange stripes. Lionel got one that looked like a bloodshot eyeball. Nancy got a green shooter with sparkles inside.

"No fair! Yours is prettier than mine," Grace said to Nancy, and pushed in front of her. "Can I go first, Mr. D? Can I?"

"Whoa, no pushing. Everybody will get a turn."

Shooting marbles was harder than it looked. Nancy didn't get any points.

"Don't feel bad," Bree said. "I stink too."

When it was almost time to go home, Mr. D scooped up the little marbles. Then he passed a bag around to collect the shooters.

"Hey! Watch this." Lionel held the eyeball marble between his thumb and his pointer finger. He made a fist and rubbed both his hands together. When he opened them, the eyeball marble was gone.

"Pretty good trick!" their teacher said.

"It's not a trick," Lionel insisted. "It's magic."

"Then do some more magic and make it reappear." Mr. Dudeny waited until Lionel dug inside his sleeve for the marble.

"Aw, rats," said Lionel. "I wanted to keep it."

Mr. Dudeny was retaping the beautiful blue shooter to the table when the bell rang.

"Adios, Dudes. See you tomorrow on Family Day."

CHAPTER **5**

THE
RETURN OF
RHONDA

efore dinner, Nancy was at Headquarters. She was reading about how
to make disappearing ink. Suddenly the
curtain parted. She expected to see Bree.
Instead, there was Rhonda.

"Uh, hi, Nancy. Your mom said you were

41

out here. Um, look, I"—Rhonda shifted from leg to leg—"I came over to tell you something."

Well, this was an interesting development! Had Rhonda come to confess?

Nancy smiled an encouraging smile. She waited for Rhonda to drop to her knees and start sobbing about the horrible thing she'd done. And because Nancy was so kindhearted, she'd say, "Of course I forgive you, Rhonda."

"Uh, look, Nancy . . ." Rhonda seemed about to blurt something out but then stopped. When she spoke, all she said was, "Want to come over and play soccer? My dad just set up a goal in our yard."

What? So Rhonda wasn't here to confess? Then she must have come over to lure Nancy into the trap!

"It'll be fun," Rhonda said.

Oh, right! It'll be a ton of fun to fall into some hole you dug. So a hundred years from now, a kid will be playing in your yard and discover a bunch of bones—my bones!

"No," Nancy said. "Maybe some other time." *As in, never!*

"Well, then—uh, bye, I guess," Rhonda said.

"No, wait!" Nancy pulled Rhonda inside and sat her in one of the beanbag chairs. Now was her chance to make Rhonda talk.

"Stay. Have a snack." She handed Rhonda a bag of cookies. On TV shows detectives sometimes got suspects to blab by acting really friendly. Nancy figured she'd give it a try.

"It sure is great to see you, Rhonda," Nancy said.

"Huh? You see me all the time." Rhonda nibbled on a cookie.

"I know. But it's always great." Nancy paused. "That's because we're friends, right?"

"Yeah, sure." She took another cookie

and stood up. "I better get home."

Nancy had to think fast.

"Look, Rhonda. I don't think you came here because you wanted to play soccer. Tell me why you really came over."

Rhonda avoided Nancy's eyes. "I—I don't know what you're talking about."

"Oh, I think you do," Nancy said.

Suddenly Rhonda slumped back down in the beanbag chair. Nancy poured a glass of water and handed it to her.

"Make it easy on yourself, Rhonda, and tell me the real reason you came over. I can tell you want to confess."

Rhonda took a sip. "Well—" She started to speak when Nancy's mother barged into Headquarters.

"Your mom called," she told Rhonda. "She wants you home."

Rhonda sprang from the chair. "See you!" she cried, and was gone.

"I was working on a case, Mom. I was about to crack it wide open when you came in."

"My bad, Sherlock. . . . Listen. I bought strawberries for dessert. Want to help make whipped cream?"

"I guess." Nancy followed her mother to the kitchen. How come Nancy Drew never ran into the problems that Nancy Clancy did, trying to solve a mystery?

Of course, Nancy Drew didn't have a mother. There was just her father, Carson Drew, and a kindly housekeeper named Hannah. Nancy felt sorry for Nancy Drew not having a mother. But maybe Mrs. Drew would have messed up her cases too.

CHAPTER 6

CRIME SCENE

"**H**urry, honey!" Nancy's mom called.

"Mom, I can't find one of my bracelets." Nancy needed it to complete her outfit for Family Day.

"Really. It's time to go," her mom said. "We don't want to be late."

Nancy came downstairs, and right away

she saw the bracelet she'd been looking for.

It was on JoJo's wrist.

Nancy pointed. "That's my bracelet!"

"Sorry!" JoJo said. Right away, she took off the bracelet and went to get her jacket.

"She always takes stuff without asking," Nancy said to her parents.

"Don't be mad, Nancy." JoJo clasped her hands together. "Please don't be mad."

"Okay, okay," Nancy said.

On the walk to school, JoJo slipped her hand into Nancy's and skipped the whole way.

The Clancys were among the first to arrive in room 3D. After saying hi to Mr. D, Nancy steered her parents to the mementos table.

"Voilà!" She pointed to her chunk of pyrite. "I hope you'll find my paragraph enthralling."

Before long, the classroom filled up with families. Bree had brought a disposable camera. So Nancy posed like a model by her chunk of fool's gold. Then Nancy took a photo of Bree with her glass mouse. Then Bree took a photo of JoJo and Freddy together.

Lionel was dragging his parents over to see the witch potato.

"Smile, Lionel," Bree said.

"Wait!" Lionel said, holding up the potato. "Okay, now!" Lionel's tongue was hanging down on his chin. His eyes were rolled so far back, all you could see were the whites.

"Stop that, Lionel!" his mother scolded. "Nobody else is acting silly."

Nancy's mom and dad looked at each other and smiled.

"What?" Nancy asked.

Her father nodded at Lionel. "That was me, twenty-five years ago. The class clown."

Bree snapped more pictures of kids and their mementos. Then they joined a bunch of kids at the snack table while Mr. Dudeny talked to the parents.

"I am so glad we could share our mementos with you," he said. "This is part of our unit on families. Earlier in the year, we made family trees. Soon each child will begin writing an autobiography. In art they will make family collages, and in . . ."

Nancy tuned out the rest of what Mr. Dudeny was saying. She watched JoJo and smiled. JoJo was taking Yoko's little sister around the memento table. Hariko was only three. JoJo was holding her hand and pointing out different stuff to her. It was like JoJo was pretending to be a big sister.

Deep down, Nancy was glad JoJo had come to Family Day. She hugged her sister when it was time for all the families to leave.

"*Au revoir!*" Nancy said, waving.

Bree kept snapping photos all day—at lunch, in the school yard, during art, and lots more in their classroom.

"One left," she said. Her desk was next to Nancy's.

"Take another of me." Nancy had her creative-writing journal out. She put a dreamy look on her face and held a pencil with her pinky finger up. "Do I look creative?"

"Bree!" Mr. Dudeny said. "Please put the camera away and get to work."

Nancy loved creative writing. She was writing a mystery called "The Vanishing Jewel." It starred a young detective named Lucette Fromage. Lucette had long, curly tresses. "Tresses" was such a beautiful word for hair. Lucette was also the same age as Nancy.

Lucette Fromage sprinted after the robbers, Nancy wrote. Mr. Dudeny liked vivid—that meant colorful—words. "Sprinted" was way more vivid than "ran."

"Be careful, Lucette Fromage!" the countess shouted from the steps of her mansion. "My sapphire blue ring is priceless. But I don't want you to get maimed."

The robbers laughed like maniacs. "You'll never catch us!" Then they drove off in an ugly used car.

It was hard trying to write the chase scene. Lucette was too young to drive. Ah! Nancy decided to give Lucette really fast, strong legs. *Lucette hopped on her bike and began pedaling at seventy miles an hour,* Nancy wrote. *Soon she was right behind the robbers.*

At one point, Nancy turned around and looked up. Mr. Dudeny was standing behind her desk. He was reading over her shoulder. "Superb!" he said.

"Dudes, listen to all the vivid words Nancy has used," Mr Dudeny said.

Nancy read out loud to the class. She explained that "priceless" meant really expensive and "maimed" meant hurt. Then she said, "At first I was going to make the stolen ring be a diamond ring. But I changed it to a sapphire after seeing Mr. Dudeny's beautiful blue marble."

"Hey! Look!" Grace said in surprise. She was pointing to the mementos table.

The crisscrossed pieces of tape were still stuck on the table. But the marble was gone.

"No worries. It must have gotten unstuck and rolled off," Mr. Dudeny said. "Let's search."

Grace checked the wastebaskets. Yoko, Lionel, and Tamar went through the book bins in case the marble had dropped into one. Nancy and Bree searched under the radiators. Nancy saw a dead bug, but no marble.

"It's not in Eric Clapton's cage, either," Clara said. "I checked."

Grace rolled her eyes. "Cla-ra! How could that huge marble get inside the hamster's cage?"

"I don't know. But I checked anyway." Clara looked upset. "How could it have disappeared?"

"I'm sure it'll turn up," Mr. Dudeny

kept saying.

"I think somebody stole it!" Grace said, in a low voice so Mr. D couldn't hear.

"You think she's right?" Nancy asked Bree.

"It does seem suspicious."

"Then our classroom might be a crime scene!" This struck Nancy as both thrilling and upsetting.

Right before going home, Bree aimed her camera at the mementos table. "Maybe we can get the pictures back today." She paused and snapped her last picture. "Who knows? There could be a clue!"

Ooh la la! Now Nancy and Bree had two mysteries to solve—the Secret of the Twins . . . and the Case of the Missing Marble!

CHAPTER 7

HUNTING FOR CLUES

Bree's mom came back with the photos late that afternoon. The girls looked through them at Sleuth Headquarters.

Bree giggled. "Look at Lionel."

Nancy was busy studying some other photos. "I am trying to establish the time of the crime." In sleuth talk, establish meant figuring out something.

"These two photos are clues." Nancy handed Bree one of Bree's parents at the display table. "See the clock on the wall?"

"Yeah. It says eleven," Bree said.

"The blue marble is still there." Nancy held up a different photo. "Now look." Everybody except Bree was standing behind the display table. Mr. Dudeny was in the photo too. But the marble was gone.

"Ooh, I have goosebumps!" Bree said.

"Me too! Too bad the clock got cut off in this one."

"Doesn't matter," Bree said. "I remember I took it right after lunch."

"Hmmm. Lunch is over at one fifteen. So that means the marble disappeared sometime between eleven and one fifteen." Nancy heard herself and stopped. "Oh, Bree! We are really sleuthing! Nancy Drew would be so proud."

Bree flung her arms around Nancy. "Partner, we are going to crack this case wide open!"

* * *

At dinner that evening, Nancy's dad said, "My, my. Just the other day you were complaining about the lack of crime around here." He paused to spoon some carrots onto his plate. "And now look! Grand theft at school!"

"Doug, stop teasing," her mom said.

"Looks like an inside job to me," her dad went on, ignoring a loud sigh from her mom.

"I don't feel good. My tummy hurts." JoJo climbed into Mom's lap.

Nancy's dad turned to her and said, "So? Was anybody ever alone in the classroom?"

Nancy had already thought about that. "No. Only Mr. Dudeny. He stays in while we're at recess."

"Hmmm. Doubtful he stole his own
marble . . . unless, of course, your teacher
is losing his marbles." Her dad laughed at
his own joke. Her mother shook her head
and carried JoJo upstairs to lie down until
she felt better.

Later that evening, Nancy lay on her bed, pondering. Pondering was like thinking, only fancier. Next to her on her night table was *The Witch Tree Symbol. How would Nancy Drew go about solving the Case of the Missing Marble?* she wondered.

Nancy picked up the book and opened it.

She didn't expect to find any answers in it. She just liked looking at the first page. In the top corner it said *Marjorie Sneff* in curly script. That had been Mrs. DeVine's name when she was a child in days of yore.

"*Sacre bleu!*" Nancy said out loud. In French that meant "Oh my gosh!"

There was a dark brown fingerprint by Mrs. DeVine's name. It had never been there before. And the page was torn.

"JoJo!" Nancy hollered. She charged into her sister's room. JoJo was on the floor, playing with all the things in her plastic treasure chest. Evidently her tummy felt all better. She was eating an Oreo. Dark brown crumbs were all over her mouth and fingers.

She looked up, saw Nancy, and snapped

her treasure chest shut.
She had a guilty look on
her face.

"You're not allowed to
touch my stuff!" Nancy
shoved the open book
at her sister. "Look what you did!"

"I didn't do that!"

"You did too! Look at your hands. This
fingerprint was made by someone eating
an Oreo cookie!"

Quickly JoJo hid her hands behind
her back. "It wasn't me! I don't like those
books. They're scary."

Nancy ran to find their mother. She was
halfway down the hall when she stopped.
Maybe JoJo was telling the truth. The covers
of the Nancy Drew books did scare her.

Nancy examined the fingerprint in the book more closely. It was big. It was probably a thumbprint.

"Come with me," she told JoJo. They went into Nancy's room. Nancy took her sister's hand and pressed her thumb onto a page in her detective notepad. A brown thumbprint appeared. It was the same color as the thumbprint in the Nancy Drew book. But it was much smaller.

JoJo was innocent after all.

"I'm sorry I blamed you," Nancy told her.

"That's okay," JoJo said. "Will you read to me?"

"Yeah, I guess."

They went back to

JoJo's room. JoJo pushed her treasure chest under her bed and found her favorite book. She handed it to Nancy. It was about a pirate ship and buried treasure.

The whole time Nancy was reading, she kept thinking about the brown thumbprint in her book. Who besides Bree and JoJo had been in her room lately?

Ooh la la! It hit her. The twins! They had come over a few days ago after soccer. Had Rhonda been eating anything chocolatey? No, Nancy didn't think so. But maybe the thumbprint wasn't chocolate. Maybe it was dirt! That made sense. Everybody came back from soccer all muddy. Nancy never would have let Rhonda touch the Nancy Drew book with dirty hands. So when did Rhonda commit the crime?

Suddenly Nancy remembered. Mrs. DeVine had called about coming for tea. While Nancy was on the phone, the twins were alone in her room. Double ooh la la! All the pieces of the puzzle were falling into place. Rhonda had probably picked up the Nancy Drew book just to look at it, and messed it up by mistake. Rhonda was scared to confess. And so Rhonda made Wanda promise not to tell Nancy.

It all made sense. Still, Nancy had no proof. On TV, detectives always talked about fingerprint files. If a fingerprint was found at the scene of a crime, they could match it up with one in the files.

The trouble was, Nancy didn't have any other fingerprints of Rhonda's. . . .

Or did she? Rhonda had been at

Headquarters just yesterday. The glass of water!

Nancy flew downstairs.

"Wait! You didn't finish!" JoJo called.

Nancy grabbed her trench coat and a flashlight from the pantry. Her father was loading stuff into the dishwasher.

"Where are you going?"

"To Headquarters. I'll be right back."

Outside, Nancy clicked on the flashlight. She made her way under cover of darkness. Inside Headquarters, the glow from the flashlight cast spooky shadows.

There it was. The plastic glass with Tinker Bell on it. Nancy held it at the bottom so she wouldn't get her own prints on it.

Once she was back in the kitchen,

she put the Tinker Bell glass on a counter. Then she turned to her father. "Dad, whatever you do, don't touch that glass! It's evidence!"

"Whew! Lucky you warned me!" he said.

There was no time for the Special Delivery mail basket. Nancy called Bree. She filled her in, then asked, "See if your mom will let you come over. And bring the kit!"

Bree's aunt had sent her a Junior

Detective kit for her birthday. It had all sorts of superb stuff, including a bottle of fingerprint powder.

"This is so thrilling!" Bree said as she burst into the Clancys' kitchen. "I can't believe we're going to dust for prints."

Nancy's father stood by, watching. "Whatever it is, I swear I'm innocent! I'm a law-abiding man with a wife and children."

"Very funny, Dad," Nancy said as he left the room. She put on a pair of yellow rubber kitchen gloves. "This way no more prints will get on the glass." Very carefully she picked up the Tinker Bell glass. Bree sprinkled on some fingerprint powder.

Sure enough, five white, powdery fingerprints appeared. Bree was peering at the biggest one with the little magnifying glass from her kit. "Here's the thumbprint."

They took the glass upstairs. Nancy showed Bree the brown fingerprint in her

Nancy Drew book.

"Now comes the test," Nancy said. Using her jeweled magnifying glass, she studied both thumbprints. So did Bree.

"Definitely a match!" Nancy said. "The thumbprints are identical! We have solved the Secret of the Twins. Just like real detectives."

Bree said, "So what happens next?"

The answer was obvious. "We solve the Case of the Missing Marble!" Nancy said.

"No, that's not what I meant. Will you confront Rhonda with the evidence?"

"Oh!" Nancy sank down onto her bed. "I have to think about it. . . . Rhonda should have just told me. I would have been mad. But not that mad."

CHAPTER **9**

INNOCENT!

Nancy's mom was wrong about the janitor finding Mr. Dudeny's blue marble.

"Still missing," Mr. D said when Nancy asked the next morning.

The missing marble was all anybody

could talk about before the bell rang.

"Dudes, come on! It is only a marble," Mr. D told the class.

"But it was your mystery memento!" Yoko said.

"It was very beautiful!" Clara said.

"Your grandpa gave it to you!" Robert said. "That's important."

"The memories I have of my grandfather are what's most important. I'll have those forever. Listen. I hope the marble turns up. But let's not overreact. . . . Now please get out your spelling books."

Nancy opened her desk to get her book. Instead she got a nasty surprise.

There was a piece of lined paper with a message.

I THINK YOU STOLE THE MARBLE!

Nancy was so shocked, she jumped back in her seat.

"What? Is there a mouse?" Clara asked.

Nancy didn't answer. She was still staring at the note. How dare someone accuse her of stealing!

Mr. Dudeny came over to her. "Is something wrong?"

Nancy nodded.

Mr. Dudeny took her outside into the hall.

Nancy showed him the message. It was written in green marker in big capital letters. The marker was going dry, so the letters looked like they were disappearing. It made the message look even meaner, and scarier, too.

Mr. Dude's lips were pressed together tightly.

"I swear I didn't take it, Mr. D!" Nancy felt tears start to prick her eyes.

"Nancy, of course you didn't. I don't think anybody took it. But I'd never, ever think that of you. You are a girl with a lot of integrity."

"*Merci*, Mr. D." She wasn't sure what integrity meant. But she could tell it was good.

After she returned to her seat, Mr. Dudeny held up the message. "This was in Nancy's desk."

Several kids gasped.

"Oh! That's so mean!" Clara said.

"Nancy is innocent!" Bree cried. She reached over and squeezed Nancy's hand.

"Clara is right. This is very hurtful. From

the first day of school, we have talked about respecting one another's feelings. I expect the person who wrote this to come see me before the end of the day." Then Mr. Dudeny put the note in his desk.

He told the class to put away their spelling books. Instead, he got one of the books from the reading nook. "It's called *Thick and Thin.* And it's about friends trusting one another."

The story was about a boy who got into trouble after finding a twenty-dollar bill in a parking lot. Nancy couldn't pay attention. She kept saying to herself, *Somebody thinks I'm a thief.*

At one point Mr. Dudeny looked up from the book and said, "Grace, please stop doodling and listen."

"I am. I can do both at once," Grace answered.

Mr. Dudeny went over to Grace's desk. He crumpled up the piece of paper and tossed it into the wastebasket. Then he picked up the book again.

Throughout the morning, Nancy kept thinking about the message. By the time it was recess, she was way more than mad. She was furious. She felt outraged!

"Come on," Bree said. "If we run we can claim the top of the jungle gym before the fourth graders get it."

"Go ahead. I'll come in a second."

The classroom cleared out fast. Mr. Dudeny was at Clara's desk, going over her math problems. Clara often needed extra help.

On the way out, something made Nancy fish the crumpled piece of paper from the wastebasket. It was just a hunch.

Grace's doodles were in green marker. The marker was almost all dried out.

Nancy stormed outside to the yard. She spotted Grace over near the slides. She was jumping rope. A bunch of first graders were watching her and counting off the jumps.

"Sixteen . . . seventeen . . . eighteen . . ."

Nancy waited until Grace lost her turn. Then Nancy cornered her. "It was you! You stuck that mean note in my desk!"

Grace blinked. "Says who?"

"Me. This"—Nancy shoved the doodle at Grace—"and the note are both in green marker, a green marker that is almost dry."

Grace looked caught for a second. Then she said, "Well—well, I wasn't trying to cover it up, so there. I don't care if you know it's me. I still think you're the thief."

"Why didn't you just say it to my face?" Then Nancy paused. "What makes you think I took it?"

"You kept saying how beautiful the marble was. . . . And that story you wrote, about the sapphire ring that got stolen."

Even to Nancy, it kind of made sense that Grace figured she was the thief.

"You wanted Mr. D's marble. So you took it!"

"I did not, Grace. Who knows? Maybe you did. And—and you're just trying to throw the blame on me."

Grace's mouth dropped open.

Ha! Got you, Nancy said to herself. Yet she didn't like how hard and mean she sounded.

"That's crazy!" Grace said. Her hands were on her hips. "Some dumb baby marble. Why would I want it?" Then all of a sudden Grace got a funny look on her face. "Are you going to blab to Mr. Dudeny about me putting the note in your desk?"

"I'm not a tattletale. But you better tell him."

Grace shrugged. "Okay." Then she went back to wait for another turn at jump rope. Grace was an expert at jumping rope. She could do a perfect split. She was a great speller. And she never lost blinking contests. Still, Nancy wouldn't ever want to trade places with Grace.

"Nancy! Over here!" Bree, Tamar, and Clara called from the top of the jungle gym.

Nancy ran off to join her friends.

CHAPTER 10

SUSPECTS

"Okay. Let's get down to business," Bree said that afternoon. "We need to draw up a list of suspects."

They were in Bree's room. Nancy was staying at Bree's until her mom and JoJo came home.

WHO STOLE THE BLUE MARBLE? Bree wrote at the top of a page in her notepad. Bree had gorgeous handwriting—her capital Bs were especially lovely.

Lionel, Bree wrote. She looked up at Nancy. "I put him down because he likes to play tricks. Maybe he took the marble as a prank."

Nancy shook her head. "Lionel wouldn't go that far. Lionel's a goofball, but I don't think he took the marble."

"Yes, you're right." Bree crossed out Lionel's name.

Nancy bit her lip and thought. On TV the crook often turned out to be the person nobody suspected. "You think maybe Clara took it?"

"Clara? That's just crazy."

"She said it was beautiful and her favorite color. . . . Who knows? Maybe some evil force came over Clara and she was powerless to stop herself." Nancy made her hands into claws. "Before she realized what she was doing, Clara snatched the marble!"

"That's just crazy," Bree repeated. "Clara never even takes a Kleenex from the box on Mr. D's desk without asking."

"What about Grace?" Nancy and Bree said at the same time. Then they both shouted, "Jinx!" The rule with a jinx was you couldn't talk until somebody said your name. And Bree was usually very strict about jinxes. But she agreed to forget about it, just this once. Solving the case was more important.

"Bree, if I tell you something, will you

keep it in the vault?" A vault was like a bank safe.

Bree shut her lips. Then she pretended to turn a key and lock her mouth.

"Grace wrote that mean message about me being the thief."

Bree gasped. "Grace is horrible. She's the worst person in our class! I bet she *is* the thief. Criminals always try to throw the blame on somebody else. That's why she wrote that message."

Nancy nodded. "I said that to her. And Grace was the one who first noticed the marble was missing."

"Well!" Bree threw out her arms as if that settled everything. "On TV shows, the person who reports a crime is always a prime suspect. . . . Plus, Grace cheats. Once she copied off my spelling test. Cheaters often grow up to be thieves. Grace just jumped from cheater to thief early."

Nancy had to admit, Bree was building a pretty solid case against Grace. Of course, they didn't have one major thing—evidence.

A few minutes later, Nancy heard her mom's car in the driveway.

"Gotta go," Nancy told Bree. "I really feel like we're closing in on this case."

CHAPTER **11**

CONFESSION

ancy burst into her house.

She found her mother upstairs. She was holding a thermometer.

"Mom, you won't believe what Grace did!" Then Nancy told her the story.

"You're right. I can't believe it!" She cupped Nancy's face in her hand and kissed her forehead. Then Nancy's mom asked, "Does your teacher know about this? Maybe I should speak to Grace's parents?"

"No, don't! Grace confessed to Mr. Dudeny. He's taking care of it. He told me before I left school. You don't need to call anybody! Promise!"

"Okay, okay. I promise."

"At first I felt awful. But all day long, kids in my class kept coming up to me. They all said how they knew I'd never steal anything." Nancy paused. "I never realized I had so much integrity."

Her mom wrapped Nancy in a hug and planted another kiss on her forehead. "You sure do, kiddo!"

Nancy followed her down the hall to JoJo's room. JoJo was in bed. "Your teacher said you were fine all day." Mom bent down and stroked JoJo's cheek. Then she turned to Nancy. "As soon as we got home, JoJo started complaining again about her tummy hurting." She popped the thermometer under JoJo's tongue. "Maybe I should call Dr. Cornelia."

JoJo yanked out the thermometer. *"No!"*

A moment later, Nancy's mom read the

thermometer. "No fever. . . . Maybe a little ginger ale will make you feel better?"

"Maybe." JoJo pulled the covers up to her chin.

Nancy's mom went downstairs.

Because Nancy felt sorry for her sister, she said, "Want to look through your treasures together?" It was one of JoJo's favorite things to do. Nancy started to pull out the plastic chest from under JoJo's bed.

"*No!* Go away!"

"Fine." Nancy headed back to her own room. "I was trying to be nice."

The phone started ringing.

"Nan, would you get it?"

It was Rhonda. She didn't bother saying hello. She started talking real fast. "Nancy, I got your special Nancy Drew book dirty, the one Mrs. DeVine gave you. And the page got torn. I didn't mean to. My hands were dirty. Please don't be mad. That's why I came over the other day. I was going to tell you, but I chickened out."

"It's okay, Rhonda," Nancy broke in. "I forgive you."

"You do? Oh, wow! Oh, phew! I was so worried you'd be mad. I felt horrible about it. My mom thought I was getting sick because I was acting so weird."

Nancy understood. Guilt could do horrible things to a person.

"All I can say is I'm really, really, really sorry, Nancy."

"Apology accepted!"

Nancy hung up the phone and went back to her room. She could hear her mom in JoJo's room.

"Is something bothering you?" Mom was saying. "Is there anything you want to tell me? I won't be mad."

Suddenly Nancy had a funny feeling in *her* tummy. She was thinking about what Rhonda had just said on the phone. How Rhonda's mom thought she was sick, when really Rhonda was just feeling guilty about Nancy's book.

Nancy bolted outside to Headquarters. She sat down and leafed through Bree's photos from Family Day again. She stopped at one of JoJo holding hands with Yoko's baby sister. JoJo was pointing at the marble. The next photo was of Freddy. He was by the display table too. JoJo and Hariko were off to one side. Nancy looked closer. JoJo was reaching for something on the table.

Nancy felt prickles on the back of her neck. Of course, the photo didn't prove anything. It wasn't evidence. Nancy put the pictures down and pondered. She thought about what Grace had said the other day: *"Why would I steal some dumb baby marble?"*

Most of all, Nancy thought about the way JoJo acted a minute ago when Nancy suggested looking through her treasure chest. Was there something inside it that JoJo didn't want Nancy to see?

It was like a bunch of arrows with blinking lights were all pointing straight at her sister. Taking Nancy's stuff was one thing. But taking someone else's stuff? That wasn't borrowing. That was stealing!

Nancy marched back into her sister's room. Their mother was gone. Nancy expected to find JoJo in bed. Instead she was on the floor, tying up one of her dolls.

"She was being bad. So I'm punishing her," JoJo said.

Nancy knelt down and fished around under JoJo's bed. She felt the treasure chest.

"Hey! What are you doing?"

Nancy didn't reply. She sat back on her

heels. Her heart started thumping as she raised the lid.

There it was: the blue marble.

Nancy grabbed it and charged downstairs with JoJo running after her, howling at the top of her lungs, "Stop!"

Her father had just come through the front door. Her mom was waiting to kiss him hello.

"What's wrong?" they both said.

JoJo kept screaming and trying to grab the marble from Nancy.

Nancy cleared her throat. "I'm very sorry to inform you that JoJo stole Mr. Dudeny's blue marble."

Then Nancy opened her hand and revealed the evidence.

CHAPTER **12**

CRIME AND PUNISHMENT

Nancy spread out the photos from Family Day on the kitchen table. "Voilà! See for yourself!" she said, pointing. "There's JoJo reaching for the marble. And here it is!"

"Nancy, JoJo's not on trial," her dad said. "So you can put away Exhibit A." JoJo was sitting on his lap, crying and hiccuping.

"Daddy, do you think this is funny?" Nancy plopped down in a chair. She was trying to be helpful. If her parents didn't watch out, JoJo could end up behind bars. She'd get nothing to eat but stale bread and stale water. Plus there was absolutely no way to look fancy in jail clothes.

"No, it's not funny," her dad said. "But it's not the crime of the century, either."

Nancy's mom handed JoJo a glass of water. Then her mom said, "Sweetie, why did you take the marble? You know that isn't right."

JoJo nodded miserably. Twin worms of snot were dripping down her nose.

"How about you tell us what happened," her mom said.

"Nancy will yell!"

"No, she won't," said Nancy's dad, while her mom leaned over and wiped JoJo's nose with a paper napkin.

JoJo sighed a big, heavy sigh. "I was being nice," she began. "Yoko's little sister wanted to see the marble. I tried lifting her. But she was heavy. So I picked up the marble and showed it to her." JoJo shrugged.

She acted like that settled everything.

But Nancy's dad said, "And then?"

JoJo frowned. Reluctantly, she went on. "It was so pretty, like treasure. . . . I put the marble in my pocket and took it home. I wanted to keep it in my treasure chest." All of a sudden her face scrunched up again. "I'm a bad girl! I'm a very bad girl!" she cried, and covered her face with her hands.

Nancy couldn't help feeling sorry for her little sister. Maybe JoJo had been born with no integrity and couldn't help herself.

"No, you're not a bad girl," Nancy's mom said, stroking JoJo's hair. "You're a good girl, a good girl who did something wrong. But we'll fix it. Tomorrow we'll go to Nancy's school. And you'll give the marble back to her teacher."

JoJo was not happy hearing this. "I'll let Nancy give it back."

"Me! No way!"

"JoJo, you took the marble," her dad said. "So you need to give it back and tell Mr. Dudeny how sorry you are."

Well, finally a little justice, thought Nancy, though JoJo was getting off way too easily.

So, after dinner, once her sister was in bed, Nancy marched into her parents' room. "Aren't you going to punish JoJo? I think you should."

Her dad closed the book he was reading. "Exactly what did you have in mind? A year of hard labor?"

"Ha-ha, Daddy. . . . What if saying sorry doesn't stop JoJo from stealing more stuff?"

Her mother was doing a crossword puzzle. She looked up. "It stopped you."

"Me?" Nancy pointed at herself. "What are you talking about?"

Her mom put down the newspaper. "You don't remember? You once took a rhinestone hair clip that belonged to Mrs. DeVine."

"I beg your pardon. I did no such—!" Nancy stopped cold and blinked a couple of times. Ooh, actually, maybe she did remember. "Was it shaped like a bow? And did it have pink rhinestones?"

Her mother nodded. "Yep!"

The hair clip had been on Mrs. DeVine's night table. It was magnificent! Nancy remembered trying to clip it in her hair. Then, before she knew what she was doing,

Nancy had slipped it into her pocket and taken it home. Just like JoJo. Suddenly Nancy had a terrible thought: Maybe crime ran in the family!

"I found the hair clip under your pillow. Mrs. DeVine didn't even realize it was missing until I took you to return it."

It all came back to Nancy. "I was so scared. I thought Mrs. DeVine would never want to see me again! But she gave me a hug and we had a tea party."

"And see? Did you wind up on America's Most Wanted list? No!"

"Oh, Daddy!" Nancy said. Her father could be so exasperating. But then he came over and hugged her. "In my humble opinion, you have turned into quite a splendid girl. So maybe there's hope for your sister."

Maybe her dad was right. This was what Mr. Dudeny called "food for thought." And Nancy definitely needed to ponder it more. But first she needed to do something else.

She went to her room. After a little while, she sent the Top-Secret Special Delivery mail basket over to Bree's window. In it was a message. In secret code, Nancy had written:

Oggv og cv
jgcfswctvgtu
CUCR!

Ygct aqwt
vtgpej eqcv.

To decipher the code, see page 20.

CHAPTER 13

CASE
CLOSED

"**Y**ou weren't supposed to crack the case by yourself!" Bree had on her mad face. Her lips were puckered so her mouth looked like a purse with the strings pulled tight. "We're Partners in Crime Fighting. *Partners*—that means we do stuff together."

Nancy was startled. This was not the reaction she expected. "Bree. I didn't mean to. Looking at your photos again made everything click."

Bree still looked mad.

"I'm sorry I solved the case alone," Nancy went on. "It was scary opening JoJo's treasure chest. Seeing that marble freaked me out! I wish you'd been there."

Bree's lips unpuckered a little. "The photos really were a clue?"

"A superb clue." Then Nancy said, "I bet you'll crack our next case. Then we'll be even."

Bree nodded. She was quiet for a moment. It was clear that she was pondering something. Then she said, "I'm happy JoJo turned out to be the culprit."

Now Nancy got angry. "Well, *merci* a bunch!"

"Wait. I'm not being mean," Bree answered. "But it was creepy thinking somebody in our class was a thief." She shuddered a little.

Okay, now Nancy understood. "Yes. I didn't even want it to be Grace."

Grace! Nancy would die—she would absolutely expire—if Grace found about JoJo. Nancy's mother planned to call Mr. Dudeny tonight. She promised Nancy that JoJo would confess tomorrow after everybody in the class had gone home.

"Bree, you are the only person I'm telling. My parents said I could because you are like family. But you have to swear up and down not to tell anyone."

"It's in the vault." Bree locked her lips with a pretend key.

Then they hugged and said, *"Bonsoir, chérie,"* which was French for "Good night, darling."

As they left Headquarters, Bree said, "In Nancy Drew, some evil-looking stranger always turns out to be the criminal. It's easy to tell who's bad because they've got ugly scars or sneer a lot. It's never a cute little kid like JoJo. And it would never, never be anyone in Nancy Drew's family."

Nancy Clancy giggled. "Of course not. Nancy Drew is an only child!"

This is the end of

NANCY CLANCY
Super Sleuth

Flip the book over to read

NANCY CLANCY
Secret Admirer

BOOK 2

NANCY CLANCY
Secret Admirer

BOOK 2

NANCY CLANCY

Secret Admirer

WRITTEN BY
Jane O'Connor

ILLUSTRATIONS BY
**Robin
Preiss Glasser**

HARPER
An Imprint of HarperCollinsPublishers

Nancy Clancy, Secret Admirer
Text copyright © 2013 by Jane O'Connor
Illustrations copyright © 2013 by Robin Preiss Glasser
Library of Congress Cataloging-in-Publication Data
O'Connor, Jane.
  Nancy Clancy, secret admirer / by Jane O'Connor ; illustrations by Robin
Preiss Glasser. — 1st ed.
    p. cm. — (Fancy Nancy)
  Summary: When Nancy Clancy finds out that both her guitar teacher,
Andy, and her favorite babysitter, Annie, have broken up with the people
they were dating, she decides to make them fall in love on Valentine's Day.
  ISBN 978-0-06-240364-3
  [1. Dating (Social customs)—Fiction. 2. Valentine's Day—Fiction.
3. Schools—Fiction. 4. Vocabulary—Fiction.] I. Title.
PZ7.O222Nak 2013   2012028407
[Fic]—dc23   CIP
                                                                 AC

Typography by Jeanne L. Hogle
16 17 18 19   CG/RRDH   10 9 8 7 6 5 4 3 2
❖
Bind-up edition, 2015

To Doug Stewart,
from your out-in-the-open admirer
—J.O'C.

For Garrett, Jessie's fiancé,
which is a fancy word for *not*-so-secret admirer
—R.P.G.

CONTENTS

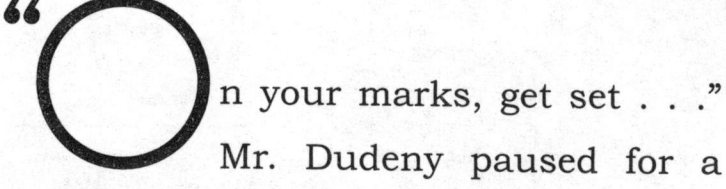

CHAPTER 1

BEATING HEARTS

"On your marks, get set . . ."

Mr. Dudeny paused for a second. "Go!"

Right away Nancy started counting. *One, two, three.* The tips of her fingers were pressed against her neck.

Four, five, six, seven, eight.

1

All the kids in room 3D were counting how many times their hearts beat in a minute. This was called taking your pulse.

Twenty, twenty-one, twenty-two.

Mr. Dudeny was watching the seconds go by on the wall clock.

Forty-nine, fifty, fifty-one.

Human Heart

For the past week, room 3D had been learning about the heart. Real hearts didn't look anything like the hearts that Nancy drew.

Seventy-two, seventy-three.

Real hearts weren't even red like the ones on Valentine's Day cards.

Eighty-five, eighty-six.

Nancy closed her eyes and tried to feel all the blood that her heart was pumping around inside her. But she couldn't feel anything. It was kind of hard to believe that she really had a heart like the one on the poster in her classroom.

"Okaaaaaay—stop!"

"My heart beat ninety times," Bree said.

"I think I got eighty-nine," Nancy said.

Robert got eighty-seven. Olivia got ninety-three.

"Me too," said Nola.

"Ha! My heart beat the fastest!" Grace shouted. "I got ninety-seven."

"This wasn't a race, Grace," Mr. Dudeny said. "And nobody's heart beats at the same rate all the time." Then he turned to Clara. "Is something the matter?"

"My heart only beat seven times!" she said.

Lionel jumped up. "Call an ambulance! This is a medical emergency!"

"Dude, sit down and stop acting silly."

Just then the bell rang. Everybody grabbed their backpacks and headed for the door. Everybody except Clara.

"Bye, Mr. Dude. See you Monday," Nancy called.

Mr. Dude waved. He was standing over Clara's desk. Nancy heard him saying, "Don't be upset. You are *not* having a heart attack. Your heart is strong and healthy." Then he took Clara's fingers and helped her take her pulse again.

Mr. Dude was the best teacher ever. Not only was he smart and funny, he was nice, too. No, he was much better than

nice: He was kindhearted!

As she walked home with Bree, Nancy thought more about that word—"kindhearted."

"We say people are kindhearted. But a heart can't really be kind, can it?" she asked.

"I guess not." Bree was busy sucking on a grape Ring Pop.

"And we call mean people heartless," Nancy went on. "Like they don't have a heart. But everybody has one."

Bree nodded. Nancy could tell that she wasn't really interested. To Nancy, however, it was important. If the heart was just some muscle, like Mr. Dudeny said, then what made people fall in love?

CHAPTER 2

GUITAR HERO

Andy arrived soon after Nancy got home. He high-fived her, then slung his guitar off his shoulder and tossed his Red Sox cap on the couch. He wore his baseball cap everywhere. Nancy thought he looked much cuter without it.

This was Nancy's sixth guitar lesson.

9

Andy was teaching her an old rock song. It was called "Wild Thing."

"What's up, JoJo?" he asked Nancy's little sister. Only the way he said it was like this: "Wazzup." That was how teenagers talked. Then Andy picked JoJo up and twirled her around and around. It looked like she was flying.

"Again!" JoJo said.

Nancy's mom came in. "Oh, no, missy! We have to leave Andy and Nancy alone."

"So?" Andy asked as he handed JoJo over to Mom. "Has my best student been practicing?"

Nancy giggled. Of course she was Andy's best student. She was Andy's *only* student. Her mom had answered an ad he had put up on the bulletin board at the

supermarket.

Nancy snapped open her guitar case. Her guitar was turquoise with little tuning knobs made of imitation ivory. It was Nancy's most prized possession. Holding the guitar neck with her left hand, Nancy began strumming with her pick. It was imitation ivory too. As she did, she switched chords from A to D to E major and back to A.

"Yesss! What I'm hearing is rock . . . and . . . roll!" Andy strapped on his guitar and started playing along with Nancy.

"Wild thing!" Andy sang. "You make my

heart sing! You make everything . . ." Andy looked over at Nancy.

"Groovy!" She sang in a low, growly voice the way Andy did.

For the next forty-five minutes Nancy kept playing. Andy showed her how to play a G chord and a C chord. Andy was a superb guitar player. And he was almost a celebrity. His band played at sweet-sixteen parties and bar mitzvahs.

"You were
totally rockin'
the joint today!"
he told her after-
ward. "With the
five chords you
know now, you can
play lots of songs."

They were drinking lemonade in the
kitchen. JoJo was sitting on Andy's lap.
She was holding his glass.

"Andy, what are you doing for Valentine's Day?" Nancy asked.

Andy shrugged. "No plans." Then he
turned to JoJo and shouted, "More lemonade!"

JoJo shook her head no.

"I want lemonade! Now!" It was a game

JoJo had made up. Andy had to act like a bratty little kid. He had to remember to say please before JoJo gave him lemonade. It was a dumb game. But JoJo thought it was hilarious.

"I think you should serenade your girl-friend outside her window." Serenade meant singing love songs to someone. It was very romantic.

"What girlfriend?" Andy asked.

"Margaret! Your girlfriend, Margaret. Remember?" Nancy had asked a million questions about Margaret. Andy's girlfriend had long brown hair, green eyes, and was almost seventeen.

"Oh, we broke up," Andy said. He didn't sound upset. But Nancy was.

"Why?"

"She said we didn't spend enough time together. I thought we spent *way* too much time together."

Nancy thought about that. "Margaret wasn't the right girl for you," she said with certainty. She finished her lemonade. "When you find that special someone, you'll never want to part."

"If you say so." Andy put JoJo down. He went and got his baseball cap and his guitar. "So? Next week, same time, same place!"

Nancy waved as he drove off in his pickup truck. She hoped Andy found the love of his life soon. Valentine's Day was only a week away!

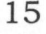

15

THE BEST BABYSITTER IN THE UNIVERSE

On Saturday night, as soon as Bree's little brother, Freddy, was asleep, Nancy and Bree had Annie all to themselves.

Annie was the best babysitter in the universe. Annie let Nancy and Bree style her hair. (It was so long she could sit on it!)

Annie gave almost perfect manicures—the polish never smooshed!—and Annie knew all the words to loads of songs.

Right now they were all dancing to a hip-hop song. Annie had awesome moves.

"Ooh! That was superb!" Nancy said. "Do it again!"

Annie spun around, stopped short, and did a hop and a kick while her arms moved up and down like a robot's.

When the song was over, they all collapsed on the sofa. Nancy was perspiring. "Perspiring" sounded more grown-up than "sweating." She was also breathing hard.

"I bet my heart is beating five hundred times a minute!" Nancy said.

"No. That's impossible," Bree said. Then she told Annie what they had learned about the heart. "Hummingbirds' hearts beat about a thousand times a minute. But not human-being hearts."

"I don't think that Nancy was being literal," Annie said to Bree. She explained that literal meant sticking to facts. That was another great thing about Annie. She knew a ton of fancy words.

At nine thirty, Annie said, "It's your bedtime. And I have to start studying for my French test."

Bree pooched out her lips. "But we didn't get to look through your fashion magazines."

"Okay, we can. But after your teeth are brushed and you're both in your pj's."

"Deal!" Nancy and Bree said together.

A few minutes later, the trundle under Bree's bed had been pulled out. Annie sat between Bree and Nancy. Slowly, they leafed through every page of *Glamour Girl,* deciding which outfits were chic. Annie said chic was French for cool. Annie said it like this: "sheek."

On page 156 was a quiz: "Is Your Boyfriend Right for You?" There was a photo

20

of a girl staring at a boy.
Over his head was a big
question mark.

"Ooh! Can we give you
the quiz?" Bree asked. "Then you'll know
if Dan is right for you." Dan was Annie's
boyfriend.

"I don't need to take the quiz. I already
know the answer," Annie said.

"Oh, that's so romantic!" Nancy clasped her hands together. "You're madly in love with Dan!"

But Annie was shaking her head. "No. That's not what I meant. Dan and I broke up. He definitely wasn't right for me."

"What went wrong?" Bree asked. "You loved his dimples and his laugh. Remember?"

"Yeah, I guess." Annie closed the magazine. "Maybe the problem was that he was too nice."

Being nice was a problem? Nancy said, "I don't understand."

Annie shut the magazine. "Oh, whatever I wanted to do was always fine with him. Whatever I said, he agreed with. It got boring."

Then Annie climbed over Nancy and blew the girls a kiss. As she turned off the light she said, "I have a date with my French book. So *bonne nuit!*"

In French that meant good night. Annie said it like this: "bun new-wee."

"I wish Annie had a real date tonight," Nancy whispered in the dark.

"Then she couldn't have come to baby-sit," Bree pointed out.

Yes. That was true. But Bree was being too—what was that word Annie had used? Too literal.

HEARTS AND MORE HEARTS

The next morning, Bree and Nancy were in their clubhouse. It was in Nancy's backyard. They had allowed JoJo and Freddy to come too.

The sign outside said SLEUTH HEADQUAR-TERS. A sleuth was a detective. And both Nancy and Bree were superb sleuths. The

file for their first case was inside a bright pink folder. It told all about catching the thief who had stolen Mr. Dudeny's big blue marble.

Nancy had bought a package of pink folders for all the cases they were going to solve. However, the other folders were still empty. Nobody seemed to be committing crimes lately. So Nancy and Bree were at Sleuth Headquarters doing homework.

Doing homework was Bree's idea. Nancy didn't see the point. Their Appreciation Hearts didn't have to be handed in until Friday.

Mr. Dudeny thought that third graders were too grown-up—"mature" was what he said—to give Valentine's Day cards to one another. Instead, everyone was making Appreciation Hearts. Appreciating someone meant liking them.

"Dudes, think of a reason why you appreciate each person in 3D," Mr. Dude had said. Then he passed out envelopes. Inside each were lots of paper hearts, along with a list of the kids in the class.

"What about kids we don't like? Can we say why we unappreciate them?" Grace asked.

"I won't bother answering that question," was all Mr. Dudeny said.

Grace. Finding something good to say about Grace was going to be a challenge.

That meant it was going to be very, very, very, very hard. Nancy lay on her back, staring up at the butterfly mobile in the clubhouse. No matter how hard she blew, it didn't move.

Already Bree had a stack of hearts finished. Nancy had only done two. For Yoko, she had written, *I appreciate Yoko because she taught me cat's cradle.* For Lionel she had written, *I appreciate Lionel because he is humorous and artistic.*

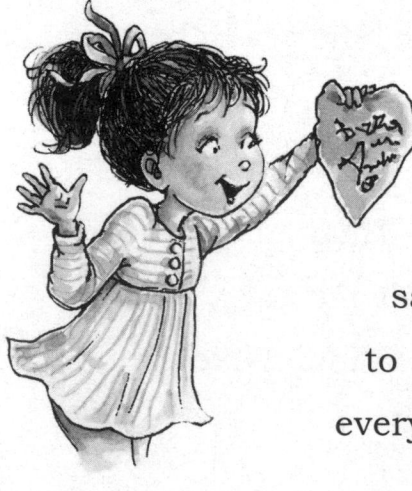

"This heart is for Andy." JoJo held up a scribble. "I love Andy." JoJo said she was going to make a heart for everybody she loved.

"Me too." Freddy put down the space guy he had been playing with. "One for Mama, one for Daddy, one for Nana." He went on making scribble hearts. "And one for Annie. When I go to bed, Annie sings to me," he told JoJo. "I love her."

All at once, Nancy sat up. She could feel an idea taking root in her mind. Andy didn't have a girlfriend. Annie didn't have a boyfriend. "Bree!" she said excitedly.

Bree didn't answer. She was checking over the class list. "Mmmm. Let's see. Whose name is next?"

Andy and Annie. Their names went together like two puzzle pieces.

Annie and Andy. It sounded like the title of a song!

Ooh la la! Nancy's idea kept growing. She could almost feel it blooming into a flower. Not just any flower, but a beautiful red rose for Valentine's Day.

CHAPTER 5

OPERATION ETERNAL LOVE

"**B**ree, stop doing homework and listen to me. Let's make Andy and Annie fall in love!"

Bree frowned as she let Nancy's words sink in. For a moment Nancy was worried. Maybe Bree thought this was a crazy idea. But a second later, Bree sprang from

the beanbag chair. She started shouting, "Yes! Yes! Yes!" and doing the little dance she did whenever she made a soccer goal. "That's the best idea ever!"

Nancy smiled modestly and said *merci*. "You think we can make them fall in love before Valentine's Day?" she asked once Bree calmed down.

"Or what about right *on* Valentine's Day!"

"Ooh. That's way better," Nancy said.

Bree had a dreamy look on her face. "Years from now, Annie and Andy will tell their kids about meeting on Valentine's Day. How they fell in love the minute they gazed into each other's eyes."

"Andy and Annie. Don't you love saying it?" Nancy imagined double hearts with

their names written in swirly letters.

"So?" Bree flopped back down in the beanbag chair. "How will we get them to meet?"

Nancy frowned. "I haven't exactly worked that part out yet."

"We need a plan."

"Yes!" Nancy said. "We can call it Operation Eternal Love." Eternal love meant loving someone forever, to infinity.

"Fine." Bree bit her lower lip. "What if I call Annie, or you could call Andy and say, 'Guess what! I know the perfect person for you. You're definitely going to fall in love. So call this number . . .'" Bree stopped. "No, that'll never work."

"Yeah, Andy's not going to call some girl because I said so. We need to arrange for them to meet someplace," Nancy said. "Only they can't know we're behind it."

Bree wrinkled her nose. "That's going to be hard."

"We'll think of something," Nancy assured her. Then she got the package of pink folders, and on the front of one

she wrote *Operation Eternal Love* in big purple letters.

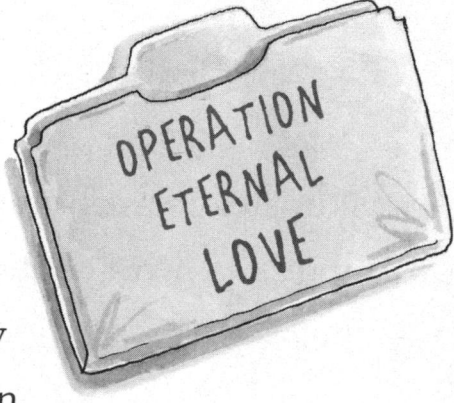

Sure enough, that very afternoon Nancy stumbled upon a plan.

Nancy was helping Dad with the grocery shopping. Before getting in line to check out, they stopped at the greeting card aisle. Her dad needed to pick out some Valentine's Day cards.

"Hey! This is a good one to give Mom!" He showed Nancy a card. There was a photo of a gorilla in a top hat and it said "I go ape for you!"

"No, Dad! All wrong! Nothing humorous!"

Instead Nancy found a card with a puffy red satin heart on the front. It said "For my beloved wife, my heart belongs to you and

only you." Then her eyes fell on another card. Ooh la la! The card was silver, and in silver glitter it said "From your secret admirer." Inside was a love poem.

"Get this one, Dad."

On the way home, Nancy asked, "What exactly is a secret admirer, Dad?"

"Hmmm. How can I explain it? It's when you love somebody but you don't tell them. Not right away. Instead, you leave presents—like flowers or poems—and write 'This is from your secret admirer.'"

That was just about the most romantic thing Nancy had ever heard!

"Were you Mom's secret admirer?" Nancy asked at home, while they were putting away groceries. "Did you worship her from afar?"

Her mom came into the kitchen and heard Nancy.

"Worship me from afar?" Mom looked at Dad and laughed. "No, sweetie. Your father didn't know I existed, even though he sat right next to me in a history class."

"Is that true, Dad?"

"If your mother says so."

Mom helped put away cartons of ice cream and packages of meat. "Then right before exam time, suddenly Dad started to notice me."

"Ooh la la! He realized you were the

girl of his dreams!"

Mom shut the freezer door. "He realized he needed help studying. Serious help."

"Were you a bad student, Dad?"

"Uh, I was more what you might call a student of life."

Nancy turned from her dad to her mom. "What does that mean?"

Nancy's mother was smiling. "It means that in college your father never missed a party and spent way too much time playing Hacky Sack."

"Team captain," her dad said proudly. "Undefeated our final season. Let's not forget that!"

"Thanks to me, you passed that history exam."

"And the rest is history!" Dad said. He

wrapped his arms around Nancy's mom and kissed her. "I never looked at another girl!"

Nancy went upstairs to her room, flopped on her bed, and pondered. Yes, her parents had found true love. But it wasn't a very romantic story. It would have been so much better if her dad had been secretly admiring her mother and then finally declared his love.

That was definitely the way Annie and Andy had to fall in love, Nancy decided. There was only one problem. How could Andy be Annie's secret admirer when he didn't even know her?

A PRIVATE CONVERSATION

Bree came up with the answer during recess on Monday. It was while she was hanging upside down on the jungle gym. Bree claimed to do her best thinking upside down. "All the blood from my heart goes straight to my brain," she said, "and makes it work better."

That didn't sound scientific. But maybe it was true. Because Bree's plan was superb. She swung right side up and explained it to Nancy.

"Every day we'll leave something for Annie at her front door. Like candy. Or a rose. And each time the note will say 'From your secret admirer.'"

Nancy was straddling a bar on the jungle gym. Hanging upside down didn't make her any smarter. It just made her dizzy. "Oh! So we're pretending to be Andy!"

"Who's Andy?" Grace asked. She was swinging from a rung above Bree and Nancy.

"This is a private conversation," Bree informed Grace.

Nancy inched closer to Bree. "Let's leave

a poem for Annie, too. A love poem!" she
whispered.

Grace climbed down a rung. "Have you
done an Appreciation Heart about me yet?"

"No," Bree said.

Nancy just shook her head. She'd finished a couple more hearts last night. But she still had a lot to go.

"I did both of yours." Then in a singsong voice, Grace said, "Want me to tell what I wrote?"

Secretly Nancy did. But right away, Bree shook her head. "No. Mr. D said it's supposed to be a surprise." Bree was much stricter about rules than Nancy.

A moment later, Mr. Dudeny called out that recess was over. That meant that Bree and Nancy had to wait until lunchtime to plan out more of Operation Eternal Love.

♥ ♥ ♥

Bree and Nancy sat at their usual table under a poster about the four food groups.

"What if we drop clues for Annie?" Bree said as she unfolded a napkin and spread it carefully on top of her tray.

"Clues?" Nancy watched Bree arrange her sandwich, milk box, apple slices, and bag of trail mix on the tray. Bree was very neat about lunch.

"Like in the first love note we say, 'My first name starts with an 'A,' just like yours,'" Bree explained. "It'll make it even more mysterious."

"Oh!" This was such a superb idea. Nancy wished she had thought of it herself. "And in another one, we say, 'I play guitar. Soon I will serenade you, my darling!'"

Bree giggled. "That's really good!"

Yoko and Clara came and sat at their table.

"Let's tell them! Please, please!" Nancy

begged Bree. Operation Eternal Love was too good to keep just to themselves.

"Tell us what?" Clara asked.

As soon as Clara and Yoko locked their lips and threw away the key, Nancy said, "We're going to make two teenagers fall in love!"

"Wow! It's like something out of a movie!" Yoko said once she heard their plan.

"I know!" said Nancy. It *was* like a movie. In the last scene, Annie and Andy would be walking down a street holding hands. . . . No, no. They wouldn't be on a street. They'd be on a beach holding hands. At sunset. Then suddenly the words "The End" would pop up over their heads.

"I don't understand." Clara had pulled

apart an Oreo cookie and was licking off the filling. "How can they fall in love if they don't know each other?"

"Simple." Nancy held up the granola bar in her lunch box to see if anybody wanted it. Nobody did. "They are going to meet on Valentine's Day."

"How?" Clara wanted to know. "Where?"

"Um, we're still planning that part," Bree said.

"You only have till Friday," Yoko pointed out.

That was true. Time was of the essence. That was something Mr. Dudeny often said. It meant there wasn't a minute to waste.

♥ ♥ ♥

After school, Nancy and Bree set Operation Eternal Love into motion. They rode over to Annie's house. No car was in the driveway. And nobody was out walking a dog.

"It looks like the coast is clear!" Nancy said. A shiver of excitement wiggled through her. This was almost like sleuthing! They parked their bikes a few houses down from Annie's. Then Nancy grabbed the love note and the granola bar from her bike basket. Nancy wished they had a fancy box of candy, the kind where each piece sat in a little pleated paper cup. But Bree kept insisting, "It's the thought that counts."

Lickety-split they dashed down to

Annie's house. As they reached the porch, a dog inside started yapping like mad. They left the note and granola bar right by the front door. Then they made a quick getaway.

On the ride back home, Nancy imagined the look on Annie's face when she read the

note. It was written on a rose-pink index card and said:

Annie, my sweetheart, you hold the key to my heart.

—From your secret admirer

Hint #1: My name starts with an "A," just like yours.

At the bottom, in silver gel-pen ink, Nancy had drawn a fancy key. Bree had written all the words because her script looked more grown-up than Nancy's.

As Nancy turned the corner onto their street, she was filled with a sense of satisfaction. Andy and Annie were one step closer to falling in love!

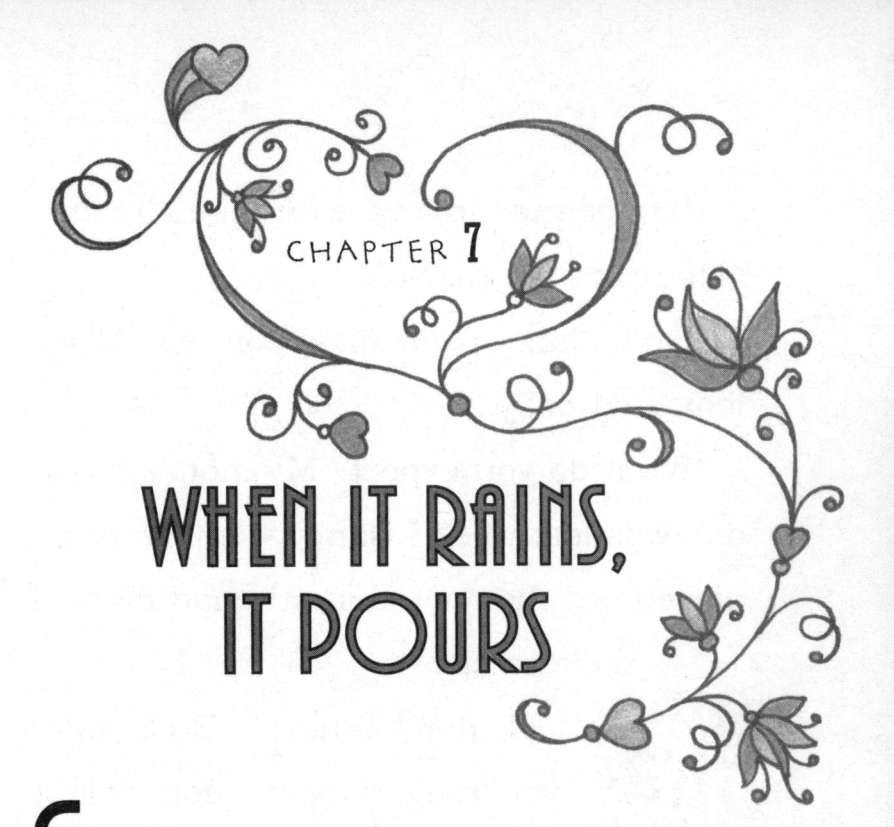

CHAPTER 7

WHEN IT RAINS, IT POURS

Step two did not go as smoothly. First it started pouring almost the minute school let out. Nancy and Bree had to run the whole way home.

Nancy was out of breath by the time they reached Bree's house. She flung herself on the sofa, panting.

Bree pointed to a vase on the hall table. "There are the roses."

"Oh." Nancy was disappointed. "They look so droopy."

"What do you expect? My mom's birth-day was last week." Nancy went over and picked out the ones that still had most of their petals.

"I don't know," Bree said, watching Nancy. "Mom might get mad."

"Don't be silly." Nancy tied her hair ribbon around the roses. "Your mom has plenty left. They're going to get tossed soon anyway."

"I guess." Bree didn't look convinced.

Then Nancy raced home and brought back the Valentine's Day card that her

dad had bought. "Here. Read this," she said, handing Bree the silver secret admirer card.

Bree read it aloud:

"No other eyes shine like your eyes.
They sparkle like stars in the night skies.
And your smile is like the morning sun,
Spreading warmth on everyone.
It's you I'm always thinking of.
To you I pledge eternal love."

"Doesn't that say it all?" Nancy smiled and sighed. "I'll get a pink index card so you can write it down."

"Oh, no! No way!" Bree shoved the card back at Nancy. "That's copying!"

Nancy sighed. "Okay, okay."

Together they came up with another
love poem.

Roses are red,
Violets are blue.
My eternal love is all
Pledged to you.

"This isn't nearly as good," Nancy grumbled.

Bree said exactly what Nancy knew she would say: "It's the thought that counts."

Nancy returned Dad's valentine, then got her raincoat, helmet, and bike. Biking to Annie's in the rain was no fun. By

the time they got there, Bree and Nancy
were soaking wet.

Once again, the house looked deserted,
which meant nobody was home.

They ran up the porch steps.

Once again, the dog started yipping.

"Aw, some of the ink ran," Bree said as they put the card and flowers on the mat by the front door. "It looks like it says 'For Amie.'"

The roses had also lost more petals.

"Nancy? Nancy Clancy?" they suddenly heard someone shouting.

Nancy and Bree spun around.

A truck had pulled to a stop right in front of Annie's house. It was Andy's old pickup truck. Inside it was Andy!

CHAPTER **8**

A CLOSE CALL

"Hey!" Andy rolled down the window. "I thought it was you!"

Nancy's brain froze. She gulped. "H-hi, Andy!"

"That's Andy?" Bree whispered. When Nancy nodded, Bree let out a squeak like a mouse. "What do we say?"

Nancy didn't know. Her brain was still frozen.

"What are you doing over here?" Andy asked. Then he pointed to their bikes. "Those yours?"

"Um, yeah. We were—uh, we were riding our bikes." Nancy licked her lips and blinked. "Then it started raining really hard. So . . . so we ducked under this porch for a minute." The words just seemed to pop out of her mouth all on their own. But they made sense. Kind of. "I have no idea who lives here," she added.

"Come on. I'll give you girls a ride home."

Oh no! Andy was getting out of the truck. What if Annie came home now? It would mess up everything!

Andy picked up both bikes and put

them in the back of the truck. Nancy and Bree scrambled into the front seat. Nancy peered down the street. So far, there was no sign of Annie.

Before Andy started the engine, he turned to Nancy. "Aren't you going to introduce me to your friend?"

"Sorry. This is Bree," Nancy said hurriedly.

"Hi." Bree smiled a nervous smile. Too many of her teeth were showing.

"Okay, away we go." Andy took out his key and started the engine. At least, he tried to. Each time, the

truck made a
funny noise.

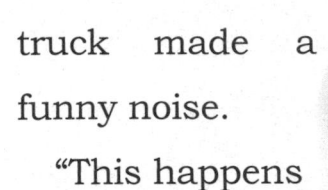

"This happens
all the time," he
said. "It'll just
take a second
to fix. Don't look
so worried, Nancy."

Worried? Nancy wasn't worried. She
was frazzled. She was frantic! She was
panic-stricken! Everything was going
wrong! While Andy got under the hood of
his truck, Nancy and Bree scrunched way
down in front so maybe Annie wouldn't
see them if she came by.

Hurry, Andy. Hurry, Andy! Nancy was
shouting in her head. Nancy was almost
100 percent positive that she and Bree

could send thoughts to each other. But they were best friends. Andy was only her guitar teacher.

At last Andy returned and—ooh la la!—this time the engine sprang to life. The truck took off down the street. At the corner, a red station wagon was waiting to make a turn.

"That's Annie's car!" Bree whispered to Nancy.

They had gotten away in the nick of time!

"Merci beaucoup!" Nancy said to Andy when they reached her house. She and Bree hopped down from the truck. "See you Friday. Same time. Same place."

"'Fraid not," Andy said as he got their bikes down. "I need to call your mom. I

got a gig late Friday afternoon." Andy was going to play guitar at the Candy Café for some little kid's birthday party.

"Oh! JoJo's going to that party!" Nancy exclaimed.

"So is Freddy—he's my little brother," Bree added.

"Maybe we can switch your guitar lesson to Saturday." Andy got back in the truck, tipped his baseball cap to Bree and Nancy, and drove off.

"Talk about a close call!" Nancy said once Andy's truck was out of sight.

Bree's hand was pressed against her chest. "My heart is pounding so hard. I have to sit down."

In the kitchen, Nancy poured two big glasses of apple juice. While she gulped

hers down, Nancy thought about what Andy had just told them. "Bree, maybe running into Andy was a stroke of luck."

"It was?"

"Think about it!" Nancy paused. "Now we know where Andy and Annie can meet Friday!"

A smile began to break out on Bree's face. She jumped up and started doing her little victory dance. "Yessss! The Candy Café!"

The birthday party invitation was on the fridge. The party ended at five o'clock.

"They always have cake at the end,"

Bree said. "Andy's gig will be over right before then."

Nancy nodded. "So around a quarter to five is when Annie has to show up. Oh, Bree, this is all working out!"

Bree said, "We can go to the Candy Café when it's time to pick up JoJo and Freddy." A dreamy look came over her face. "We can spy on Annie and Andy

and watch them fall in love!"

Nancy poured herself more juice. "Maybe it wasn't just luck that Andy drove by!" she said, squinting her eyes in deep thought. "Of all the streets in town, why did Andy pick Annie's street to drive down? Maybe he was drawn to her house like a magnet."

"Ooooh." Bree sat back and let this sink in. "It's like their love is meant to be!"

"Exactly!" Then Nancy clinked her glass against Bree's and they both said at the same time, "To eternal love!"

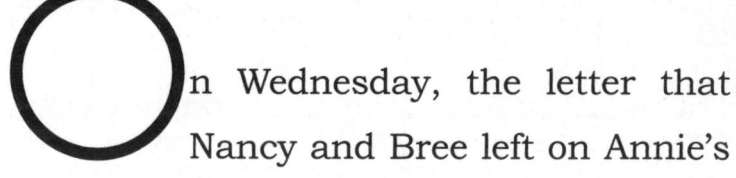

CHAPTER 9

THE
MESSENGER

On Wednesday, the letter that Nancy and Bree left on Annie's porch said:

My darling,

I cannot keep my eternal love a secret any longer. Please meet me on Friday at the Candy Café. Be there at twilight.

75

(That is 4:45.) I am tall, dark, and handsome. I will be wearing a Red Sox baseball cap.

Check one of the boxes below:

❏ *YES, I will be there.*

❏ *NO, I am not coming.*

Leave your answer at the bench by the swings at the playground.

P.S. Maybe use some tape so it won't blow away.

♥ ♥ ♥

Thursday was the longest school day ever. Nancy couldn't wait until three o'clock when she and Bree could bike to the playground. What if Annie's answer was no? Then all their hard work would have been a waste. It was too heartbreaking to think about!

Even during creative writing, Nancy's mind kept wandering. All she did was fill her paper with doodles. Little hearts. Big hearts. Hearts with frills around the edges. Inside each one were two script "A"s.

"Daydreaming, Nancy?"

Nancy looked up. "Yes. Sorry, Mr. D."

"I'm eager to find out what Lucette is up to next."

Lucette Fromage was a nine-year-old girl that Nancy had made up. In the last story, Lucette Fromage had caught a gang of jewel thieves. Now Lucette was trying to reunite a prince and the poor village girl he loved. One reason why Mr. D liked Nancy's stories was that she used vivid, interesting words, like "reunite," which meant get back together.

Mr. Dude said, "Sometimes a writer needs to daydream. Writers can get superb ideas from daydreaming."

Nancy smiled. She loved Mr. D so much. Not in an eternal-love kind of way. But because he was so wise and understanding.

At last, the minute hand crept up to the twelve and the hour hand reached the three. The bell on the wall in their classroom rang.

School was out!

Nancy and Bree jumped from their seats, raced down the hall, and burst outside. While they were stashing stuff in their bike baskets, Grace came over to them.

"Bree, your mom is parked around the corner. She told me to tell you that she's driving you and Nancy home."

"What?!" Bree and Nancy cried. "Why?"

Grace shrugged. "How should I know?"

Bree turned to Nancy. "This ruins everything."

"Ruins what?" Grace asked eagerly. "Ruins what?" she repeated, tagging along as they wheeled their bikes over to Bree's mother's car.

"Why can't we bike home?" Bree asked her mom. "We don't need you to drive us."

It turned out that Nancy's mom was working late. Bree's mom was picking up JoJo and Freddy from preschool and then doing some errands. "I don't want you girls staying in the house alone. I've got the trunk open. Put your bikes in back and jump in." Bree's mom had a

"don't argue" look on her face. Still, Bree gave it a try.

"We have to bike over to the playground," Bree said. "It's very important. Pleeeeeeeease." She strung the word out forever.

It didn't work.

"What's so important?" Grace wanted to know. "Why do you have to go to the playground?"

"None of . . ." Nancy was starting to say "None of your beeswax." Then she remembered something. Grace lived across the street from the playground.

"Grace, will you do something for us?" Nancy asked.

"Maybe. But not for free. You'll have to pay me back. Deal?"

Nancy rolled her eyes, then nodded. "Deal."

"Nancy, hurry up," Bree's mother called. Bree was already in the backseat, pouting.

Quickly Nancy told Grace what she had to do.

"Call right after!" Nancy said as she buckled up the seat belt. "I'll be at Bree's."

SWEET SUCCESS

Every time the phone rang, Nancy and Bree jumped.

At last Bree's mom said, "Bree, Nancy. It's Grace on the phone."

Bree got right down to business. "Did you find the note, Grace?"

"Yes."

"Well, does it say yes or no?" Nancy asked. It was hard sharing one phone.

"First you have to tell me what going's on."

Nancy groaned. So did Bree. But they told Grace.

"That's, like, the stupidest thing I've ever heard," Grace told them.

Nancy was about to say there was no such word as "stupidest." Instead she shouted, "Just tell us what Annie said!"

"She said no, she isn't coming!"

Bree and Nancy looked at each other. Nancy's lips trembled. Bree already had tears in her eyes.

"Ha! I'm only kidding!" Grace was laughing into the phone. "The box for *yes* is checked."

"You'd better not be kidding this time, Grace!" Bree said.

"I'll bring it to school tomorrow. You can see for yourself. And here's what you have to do to pay me back."

A minute later they hung up.

Nancy was thrilled. Andy and Annie

were meeting tomorrow! It wasn't just a plan anymore. It was really happening. She didn't even mind having Grace sit at their table at lunch for two weeks. Well, she minded, but it was worth it.

♥ ♥ ♥

At home later, Nancy practiced playing guitar. Then she finished up the last of her Appreciation Hearts. They had to be handed in tomorrow. She did Nola's and Richard's and Isabel's. In a little while there were checks by everyone's names on the class list. Everyone except Grace's. Nancy felt bad that it was so hard to find a reason to like Grace.

"Nancy. The phone is for you," Nancy heard her mom calling.

When she picked it up, she heard

Grace's voice.

"Uh, Nancy? Listen, you and Bree don't have to pay me back. The favor is for free."

What? Nancy almost asked Grace why she was being nice. Instead, she said, "*Merci*, Grace. I truly appreciate it and—and look. I guess you can still sit with us."

Nancy got off the phone. Suddenly she knew exactly what to write on Grace's heart: *I appreciate Grace because she did a favor for me.* Then Nancy put extra glitter on Grace's heart.

Just then, the bell on the Top-Secret Special Delivery mailbox started ringing.

That meant Bree was sending a message. The basket hung from a rope between their bedroom windows.

Nancy reached for the note. It was not written in code. That had to mean Bree was in a super rush to get in touch.

When she read it, Nancy understood.

The note in the basket said "Annie's baby-sitting. Come over *toute de suite!*" *Toute de suite* meant right away in French. You say it like this: "toot-deh-sweet."

Since all of Nancy's homework was done, her mom said okay.

"Guess what! Annie has a secret admirer!" Bree said the second Nancy walked in the door. Bree was hopping all around and acting excited. "Wait till you hear!"

Nancy had never realized what a good

actress Bree was. So Nancy tried to act really surprised too. "A secret admirer? Wow!" Nancy let her jaw drop open.

Annie was helping Freddy build a Lego rocket ship. "Yes! I'm meeting him tomorrow. At the Candy Café."

"Do you have any idea who it is?" Nancy asked Annie.

"Not really. He's tall, dark, and handsome and plays guitar."

"He left flowers for Annie. Roses!" Bree really sounded as if this were news to her.

"Ooh la la! That's so romantic. What did the love poem say?"

Annie looked up from the floor. "Who said anything about a love poem?"

Whoopsy! Bad slip! "Um—it's like a rule," Nancy stammered. "Secret admirers always leave a love poem."

Quickly Bree switched the subject. "Annie, how will you wear your hair tomorrow?" Then, when Annie took Freddy up to bed, Bree glared and said, "I can't believe it. You nearly blew the whole thing!"

"I'm so sorry! It just slipped out. You think she suspects?"

"No. But watch what you say!" Bree glanced at the stairs. "Shh. I hear Annie coming."

Freddy was asleep, so Bree and Nancy had Annie all to themselves now. First they took turns brushing Annie's long hair until it looked super shiny.

Then they tried out different shades of eye shadow on Annie. And different lip glosses. And different hairstyles.

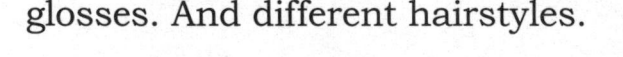

They also gave her a super-deluxe facial.

"Ummmmm. I feel like I'm at a beauty spa." Annie said.

"Ooh la la. Your skin—I mean your complexion—looks as smooth as velvet

now," Nancy said after they wiped the gook off her face.

"I'd better not get a zit before twilight tomorrow!" Annie said just as Bree's parents returned home. "Wish me *bonne chance.*" Annie said it like this: "bun shahnss." "That's French for good luck!"

TEENAGERS IN LOVE

On Friday Mr. D brought in cupcakes.

Everyone read their Appreciation Hearts. Nancy got five nices and twelve fancys.

The one Grace made for Nancy said *I appreciate Nancy because she is not boring.* Nancy read it a couple of times. Was this

a compliment? Did it mean Grace thought she was interesting?

The most special ones came from Mr. Dudeny and, of course, Bree.

I appreciate Nancy's tremendous imagination and independent spirit. She is unique—which I'm sure she knows means one of a kind.

-Mr. D

After the last bell rang, Clara invited Yoko, Nancy, and Bree to her house. But Nancy explained why they had to decline.

"At twilight Annie and Andy are meeting at the Candy Café."

"We're going to spy on them and watch them fall in love," Bree added.

"Oh, please, can we come too?" Clara begged. Nancy was ready to say yes. But Bree was firm. "Sorry. It'd be too risky with four people. Nancy and I have to stay undercover."

Bree had worked out a minute-by-minute schedule.

4:40 Arrive at Candy Café.

4:41 Go next door to Belle's Fashion Boutique.

4:42 Sneak into alleyway between Belle's and Candy Café. Spy through window.

4:43 Wait for Annie to arrive.

4:45–5:00 Watch Annie and Andy fall in love.

♥ ♥ ♥

At 4:40, right on time, Nancy's mother pulled into the parking lot behind the Candy Café.

"Can Bree and I go over to Belle's?"

Nancy's mom looked ready to say no.

"Please, oh please, Mom!" Nancy said. "It's right next door. It's not even twilight yet."

Nancy's mom relented.

At Belle's, Bree and Nancy didn't even stop to check out the jewelry counter. They went straight to the back entrance and ducked into the alley between the two stores.

The Candy Café window was higher

than they'd expected. They had to stand on their tippy toes. From the party room, Nancy could hear lots of little kids singing "Happy Birthday" to guitar music.

"Andy's gig is over now!" Nancy whispered excitedly.

Sure enough, a minute later Andy sat down at a table in the main room. A waitress took his order.

"Perfect! A table for two!" Bree squealed softly.

Now only one thing was missing.

Annie!

At 4:45 on the dot, she arrived. Annie was wearing everything they'd told her to, and she looked stunning, ravishing, breathtaking!

For a moment Annie glanced around

the room. Then she spotted Andy. Andy spotted Annie. They waved to each other.

"She's sitting down at the table! Bree, we did it. It's all coming true!"

Bree's hand was cupped over her mouth. She was speechless.

"Come on. Let's go in and say hi!" Nancy started tugging Bree by the arm.

Bree looked uncertain. "Ooh, I want to. But won't that give it away?"

"We came with my mom to pick up JoJo and Freddy. Remember? It would be rude not to say hi."

"You're right," Bree said. "But don't let

anything slip like before."

At the Candy Café in the party room, JoJo and Freddy and lots of other little kids were racing around tooting party horns. Nancy's mom was sharing a piece of cake with another mom. She saw Nancy and Bree and waved.

At a table in the back, there they were—Annie and Andy. Andy and Annie. They each were holding a spoon. In between them was a banana split. Annie was laughing at something Andy said.

It was like a movie, only better—this was real life!

Bree and Nancy went over and said hi at the same time. It came out too loud.

Andy looked up, startled. Annie swiveled around and said, "Oh! Hi, Bree. Hi, Nancy."

Andy was pointing at the banana split with his spoon. "Want to pull over chairs and help us out? This thing is huge!"

"That's very thoughtful! But we wouldn't dream of disturbing you!" Nancy said.

"You sure?" Andy asked. "We're heading to an all-dessert party later. Gotta leave some room. Right, Annie?"

Ooh la la! Annie and Andy were going to a party. Together! Tonight!

Just then, Nancy caught her mom signaling to them. JoJo and Freddy were in their coats.

"Well, got to go. See you!" Bree grabbed Nancy.

"Wait a sec." Annie stood and, wrapping an arm around Nancy and Bree, steered them to the front of the Candy Café.

"Your secret admirer is my guitar teacher! I can't believe it!" Nancy whispered. "He's tall, dark, and handsome,

just like he told you!"

"And I know for a fact that Andy isn't too nice. I—I mean he's nice, but not yucky nice, like your last boyfriend," Bree babbled excitedly.

"This is meant to be," Nancy went on. "It's love eternal. You already look like you've known each other forever!"

Annie had a funny look on her face.

"That's because we *have* known each other forever."

Bree and Nancy stopped in their tracks. "What do you mean?" they asked Annie.

"Andy and I have been buddies since ninth grade." Annie bit her lip. Then she went on. "And look, you guys. I knew you were behind the whole secret-admirer thing."

"You did? How?" Bree asked. Nancy was too shocked to utter a word.

"The writing." Annie turned to Bree. "I've watched you practice script a lot."

Nancy felt like weeping. She could see Bree did too.

"So why did you play along?" Bree asked.

Nancy was wondering the same thing.

"Because it was so sweet. You want me

to find eternal love. And . . ." Annie giggled. "I was curious to see who you picked out."

Now Nancy felt silly. Annie had been playing along, the way Andy played along with JoJo's "Say please" game. To Annie, Nancy and Bree were just dumb little kids.

Then a terrible thought struck Nancy.

"Does Andy know?" she asked. If he did, she would die; she would perish! She

would have to get another guitar teacher. And she would never play "Wild Thing" again. Ever.

Annie shook her head. "He thinks I just happened to show up here."

That was a relief. But Nancy was still confused. "But—but Andy said you're going to a party together. Isn't that a date?"

Annie shook her head. "Sorry. Andy and I are friends. It's strictly platonic." Then she hugged them both. "You guys are the best."

In the car on the way home, Nancy asked, "Mom, what does platonic mean?"

"Platonic? Hmmm, how can I describe it?" Mom said. "It means that—JoJo, Freddy, that's enough with the horns!" When JoJo and Freddy stopped tooting,

Mom started over. "It means that you like someone as a friend but not in a romantic way."

Nancy and Bree exchanged sad looks. That was what Nancy figured platonic meant. It was the first fancy word she didn't like!

"That's how it started with Dad and me," Mom went on. "We were buddies. I helped him study. Remember? I told you that. Then one weekend we went to a party together. And—I don't know. I guess love was in the air that night."

"Oh! So you went from platonic to romantic?" As Nancy took this in, she and Bree exchanged looks again. Nancy could read Bree's mind. Just like Nancy, she was thinking that maybe this would

happen to Annie and Andy. Maybe it would happen this very night!

After all, it was Valentine's Day. So love was definitely in the air!

Flip the book over to read

NANCY CLANCY

Super Sleuth

This is the end of

NANCY CLANCY

Secret Admirer